WARNING!

Scaredy Squirrel insists that everyone wash their hands with antibacterial soap before reading this book.

For Francine and Hubert

ISBN: 978-0-545-22263-1

30 29 28 27 26 25 24 23 22 21   14/0

Printed in the U.S.A.   40

First Scholastic printing, October 2009

Designed by Mélanie Watt and Karen Powers
Edited by Tara Walker
The artwork in this book was rendered in charcoal pencil and acrylic.
The text is set in Potato Cut.

Scaredy Squirrel

by Mélanie Watt

SCHOLASTIC INC.
New York Toronto London Auckland
Sydney Mexico City New Delhi Hong Kong

Scaredy Squirrel never leaves his nut tree.

the
unknown

He'd rather stay in his safe and familiar tree than risk venturing out into the unknown. The unknown can be a scary place for a squirrel.

A few things Scaredy Squirrel is afraid of:

tarantulas

poison ivy

green Martians

killer bees

germs

sharks

So he's perfectly happy
to stay right where he is.

Advantages of never leaving the nut tree:

- great view

- plenty of nuts

- safe place

- no 🦀 🍁 👾 🐝🐝 ⚛ 🌊

Disadvantages of never leaving the nut tree:

- same old view

- same old nuts

- same old place

Monday   Tuesday   Wednesday

Thursday   Friday   Saturday   Sunday

In Scaredy Squirrel's nut tree, every day is the same. Everything is predictable. All is under control.

Scaredy Squirrel's daily routine:

 6:45 a.m.	wake up	
 7:00 a.m.	eat a nut	
 7:15 a.m.	look at view	

 **12:00** noon	eat a nut	
 **12:30** p.m.	look at view	
5:00 p.m.	eat a nut	
5:31 p.m.	look at view	
8:00 p.m.	go to sleep	

BUT let's say, just for example, that something unexpected **DID** happen ...

You can rest assured that
this squirrel is prepared.

A few items in Scaredy Squirrel's emergency kit:

parachute

bug spray

mask and rubber gloves

hard hat

antibacterial soap

calamine lotion

net

Band-Aid

sardines

What to do in case of an emergency according to Scaredy Squirrel:

Dramatization

Step 1: Panic

Step 2: Run

Step 3: Get kit

Step 4: Put on kit

Step 5: Consult Exit Plan

Step 6: Exit tree (if there is absolutely, definitely, truly no other option)

Exit Plan *TOP SECRET*

Exit 1
Note to self:
Watch out for
green Martians
and killer bees
in the sky.

Exit 2
Note to self:
Do not land
in river. If
unavoidable,
use sardines
to distract
sharks.

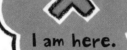

I am here.

Exit 3
Note to self:
Look out for poison ivy
and for tarantulas roaming
the ground.

Exit 4
Note to self:
keep in mind
that germs are
everywhere.

Remember, if all else fails, playing dead is always a good option!

With his emergency kit in hand, Scaredy Squirrel watches. Day after day he watches, until one day ...

A killer bee appears!

Scaredy Squirrel jumps in panic, knocking his emergency kit out of the tree.

This was **NOT** part of the Plan.

Scaredy Squirrel jumps to catch his kit.
He quickly regrets this idea.
The parachute is in the kit.

But something incredible happens . . .

He starts to glide.

Scaredy Squirrel is no ordinary squirrel.
He's a FLYING squirrel!

He feels overjoyed!

Adventurous!

Scaredy Squirrel forgets all about
the killer bee, not to mention the
tarantulas, poison ivy, green
Martians, germs and sharks.

Carefree!

score
5.7

Alive!

Until he lands in a bush . . .

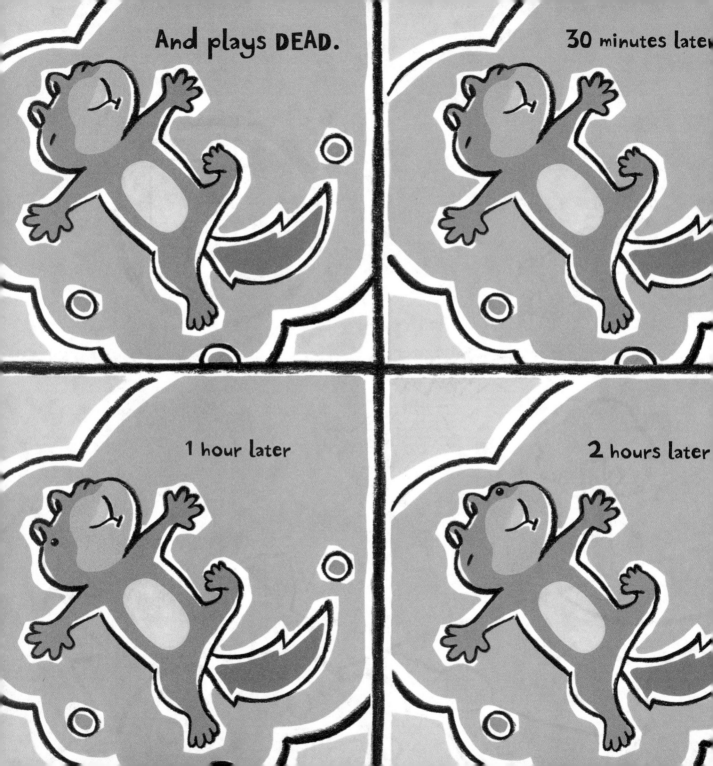

Finally Scaredy Squirrel realizes that nothing horrible is happening in the unknown today. So he returns to his nut tree.

All this excitement has inspired Scaredy Squirrel to make drastic changes to his life ...

Scaredy Squirrel's new-and-improved daily routine:

6:45 a.m.	wake up	
7:00 a.m.	eat a nut	
7:15 a.m.	look at view	
9:37 a.m.	jump into the unknown	

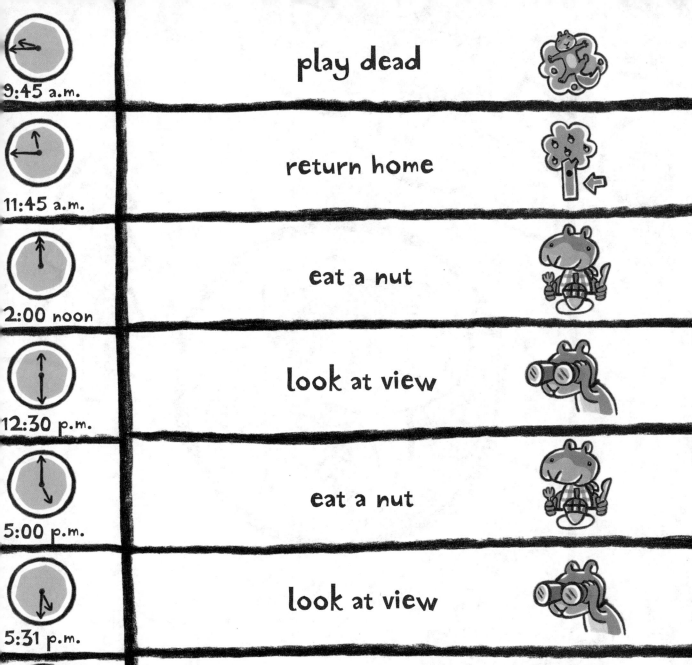

9:45 a.m.	play dead	
11:45 a.m.	return home	
2:00 noon	eat a nut	
12:30 p.m.	look at view	
5:00 p.m.	eat a nut	
5:31 p.m.	look at view	
8:00 p.m.	go to sleep	

poison
ivy

P.S. As for the emergency kit,
Scaredy Squirrel is in no hurry
to pick it up just yet.

THE
END

MÉLANIE WATT never leaves her home near Montreal, Quebec.

She would rather concentrate on creating books for kids.

Mélanie Watt's daily routine consists of waking up, eating, writing, drawing, erasing, drawing, eating and going to sleep.

Mélanie's books include:
- LEON THE CHAMELEON
- AUGUSTINE
- CHESTER
- CHESTER'S BACK!
- and Scaredy's other adventures...

P.S. Mélanie Watt is also afraid of sharks.